PARACHUTE

DANNY PARKER works as the writer in residence and director of drama at Hale School in Perth, Australia. He has written two other picture books, both of which were also illustrated by Matt Ottley. Visit Danny's website at www.dannyparker.com.au.

MATT OTTLEY has been illustrating picture books since 1983. He is one of Australia's most popular children's illustrators, and his books have been published in several different languages around the world. Visit his website at www.mattottley.com.

For my Mum. Thank you. — D.P.

For Jan Ormerod, in loving memory. — M.O.

First published in the United States in 2016 by
Eerdmans Books for Young Readers,
an imprint of Wm. B. Eerdmans Publishing Co.
2140 Oak Industrial Dr. NE
Grand Rapids, Michigan 49505
P.O. Box 163, Cambridge CB3 9PU U.K.
www.eerdmans.com/youngreaders

First published in 2013 by
Little Hare Books
an imprint of
Hardie Grant Egmont
Ground Floor, Building 1, 658 Church Street
Richmond, Victoria 3121, Australia
www.littleharebooks.com

23 22 21 20 19 18 17 16   9 8 7 6 5 4 3 2 1

Printed through Asia Pacific Offset in China

A catalog record of this book is available from the Library of Congress.

ISBN 978-0-8028-5469-8
Designed by Vida & Luke Kelly

The illustrations in this book were created on a Wacom Cintiq graphics tablet, using virtual oil paint, oil pastel, and pencil.

PARACHUTE

DANNY PARKER
MATT OTTLEY

EERDMANS BOOKS FOR YOUNG READERS

GRAND RAPIDS, MICHIGAN · CAMBRIDGE, U.K.

Toby always wore
a parachute.

It was most useful

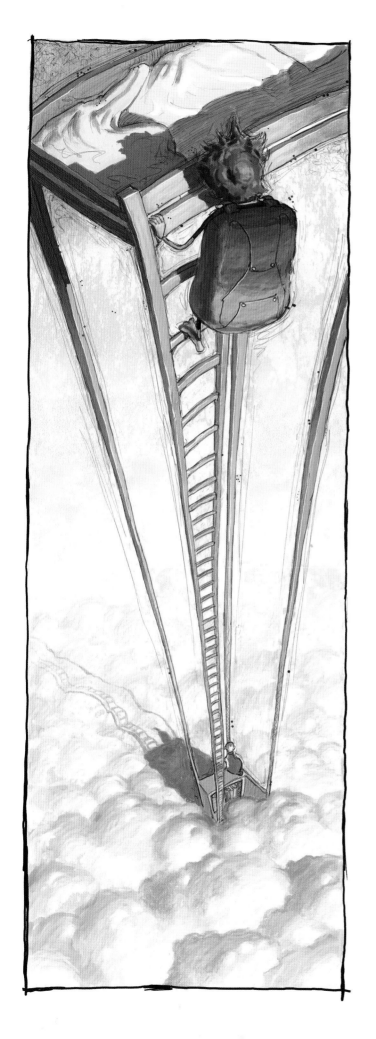

for getting out of bed
in the morning,

for when he finished breakfast,

and after he brushed his teeth.

His parachute
made him feel safe

on the swings

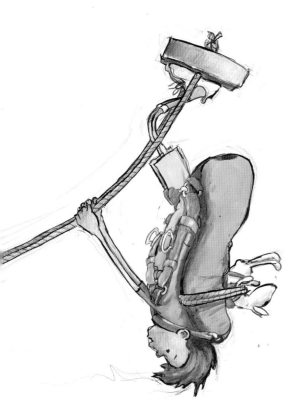

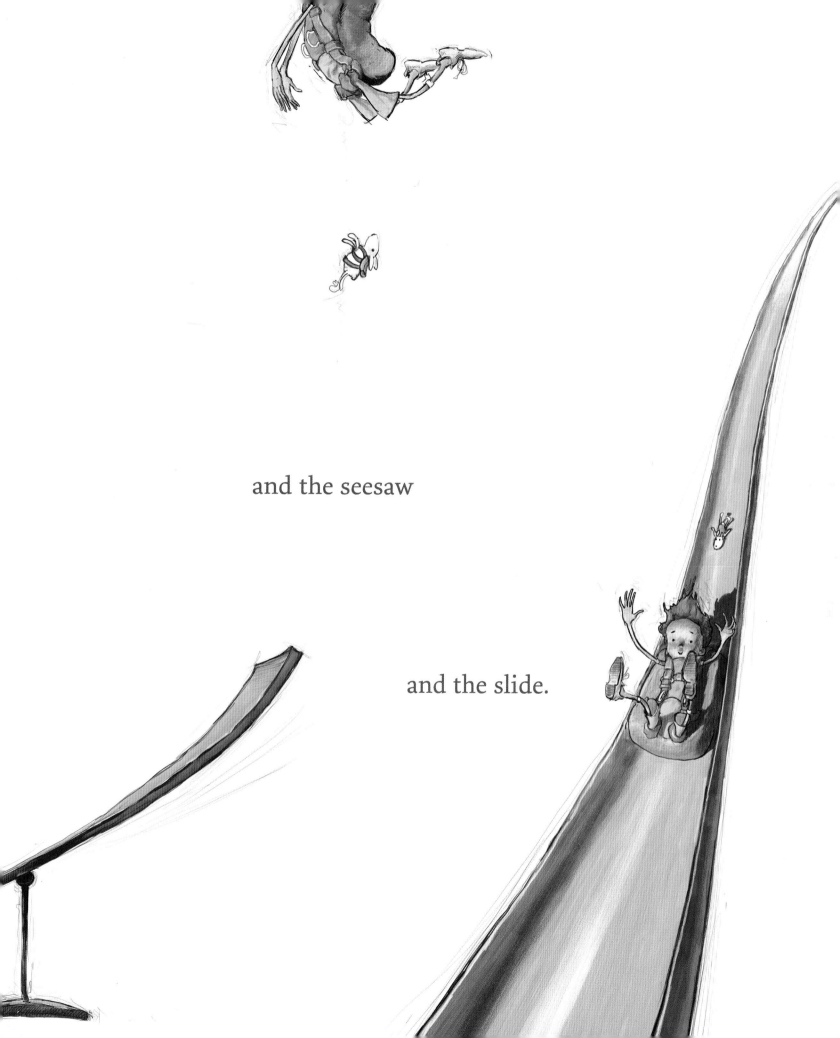

and the seesaw

and the slide.

Or whenever danger might strike.

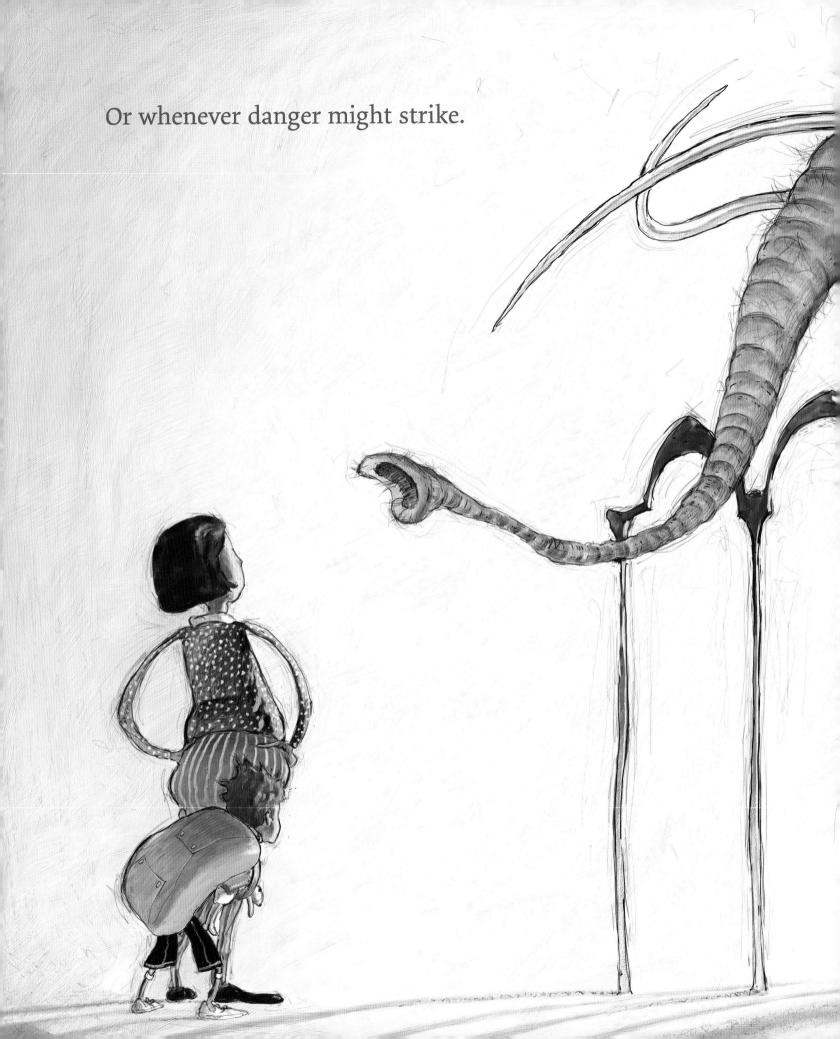

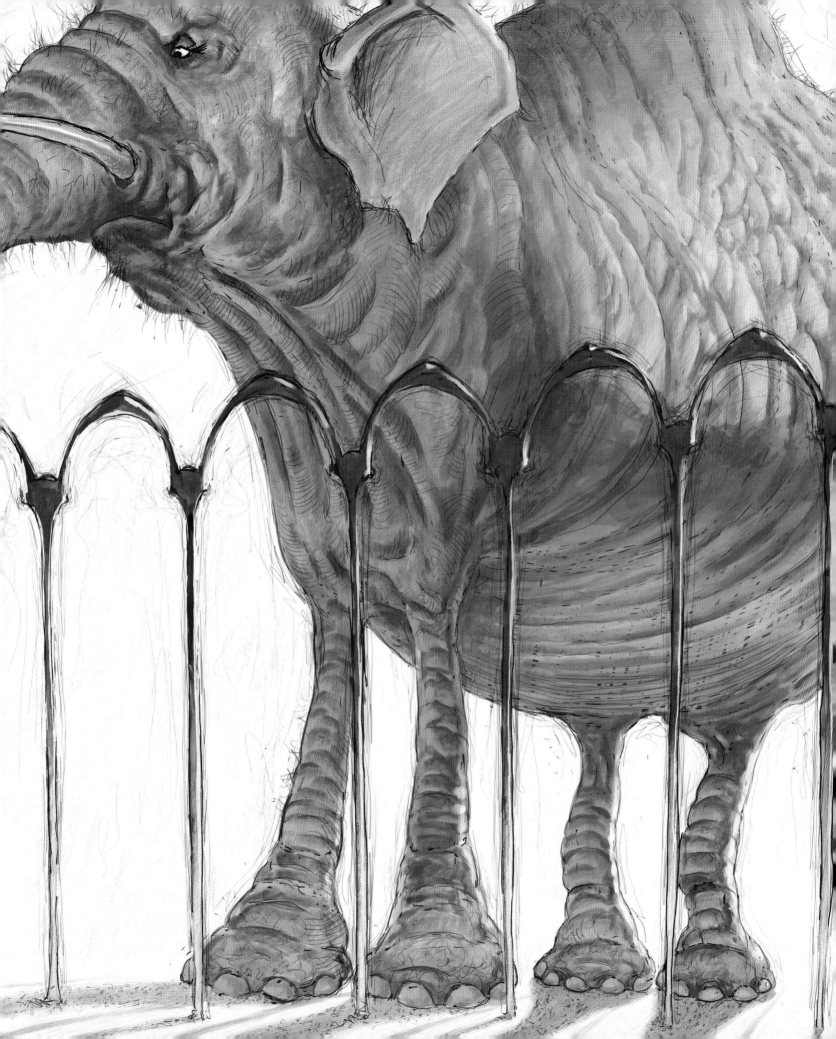

The tree house was high.

And Henry was even higher.

The ladder swung as Toby clambered up.

He didn't look down.

"Come on, Henry!" called Toby
as he reached the branch.

"Don't be scared," said Toby
as he put out his hand.

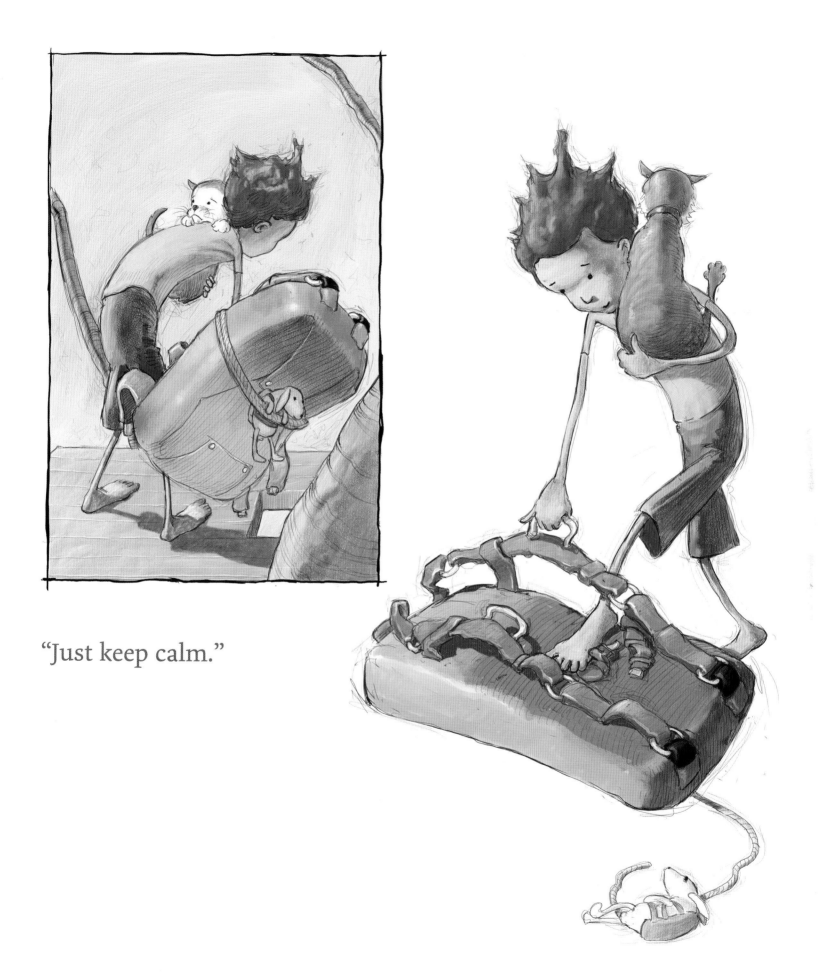

"Just keep calm."

Little by little,

Henry floated

to

the

ground.

And was safe.

Suddenly, Toby was alone.

"Come on, Toby," he said to himself.

"There's nothing to be afraid of," he said
as he held on tight.

"Just try to keep calm."

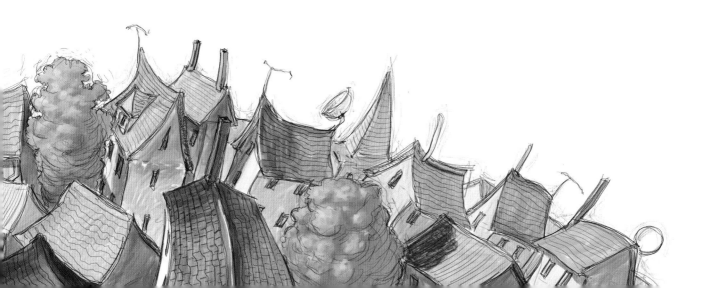

Little by little . . .

step by step . . .

Toby climbed down.

And was safe.

As time passed,

Toby needed his parachute
less and less.

And one day, he left it behind.